Our Emotions and Behavior

I'm Not Happy

Sue Graves

**Illustrated by
Desideria Guicciardini**

free spirit
PUBLISHING®

On Friday, Ben went to play at his friend Amir's house.

Amir had broken his best truck. **"I'm not happy!"** he said.

Ben wanted to help Amir.
He **helped** him fix his truck.

Amir was very happy.

In the afternoon, Ben went to play **soccer** with Tim and Lucy.

But Mike took Tim's ball.
Tim was **upset.**

Mike felt **bad.**
He gave the ball back to Tim.

They all **played** soccer together.
Everyone was **happy!**

Then Ben saw Molly and her mom. Molly was **upset.**

She was **sad** because she had lost Max, her dog.
"I can't find him anywhere!" she cried.

Ben **felt sorry** for Molly.
He **helped** her look for Max.

They looked in the bushes. But they couldn't find Max **anywhere.**

Just then, Ben's mom came along.
She said Ben had to go to his grandma's.
Please put on the sweater that Grandma
made for you," she told Ben.

But Ben **didn't like** the sweater.
It was too big and too scratchy!
Ben was **not happy.**

13

But Grandma was **delighted** to see
Ben in the sweater.

She was so **happy**, it made Ben feel **happy**, too!

Ben told Grandma about Molly's dog, Max. He told her that Molly was feeling **miserable.** Grandma had a good idea. She helped Ben make some posters.

Then they put up the posters all around the **park.**

That night, there was a knock at
Ben's door. It was a man . . .

18

. . . and he had Max with him! The man told Ben he had seen the posters. "Then I saw Max!" he said.

Everyone was **happy** . . .

. . . but Max was the **happiest of all!**

Can you tell the story of what happens when the boy's balloon flies away?

How do you think he felt when he lost his balloon?
How did he feel at the end?

A note about sharing this book

The **Our Emotions and Behavior** series has been developed to provide a starting point for further discussion about children's feelings and behavior, in relation both to themselves and to other people.

I'm Not Happy
This story explores in a reassuring way some of the typical situations that can make people unhappy. It explores how we can help ourselves feel better when we are sad, and how we can make others feel better.

The book aims to encourage children to have a developing awareness of their own needs, views, and feelings, and to be sensitive to the needs, views, and feelings of others.

Picture story
The picture story on pages 22 and 23 provides an opportunity for speaking and listening. Children are encouraged to tell the story illustrated in the panels: the little boy is sad when he accidentally knocks into the girl and his balloon flies away. He is cheered up when the girl helps him get his balloon back.

How to use the book
The book is designed for adults to share with either an individual child or a group of children, and as a starting point for discussion.

The book also provides visual support and repeated words and phrases to build confidence in children who are starting to read on their own.

Before reading the story
Choose a time to read when you and the children are relaxed and have time to share the story.

Spend time looking at the illustrations and talking about what the book may be about before reading it together.

After reading, talk about the book with the children

- What was it about? Have the children ever felt unhappy? What made them unhappy? Have they ever broken a favorite toy? Who helped them feel better and how?

- Talk about Tim's and Molly's experiences in the story. Have the children had similar experiences? Encourage the children to take turns sharing their experiences with the others and to listen without interrupting.

- Talk about Mike taking Tim's ball away and how this made Tim sad. Do the children think that this made Mike feel happy? How did Mike make Tim feel better? What would children do if they made someone feel unhappy? Talk about the importance of saying "I'm sorry."

- Extend this discussion by talking about other occasions when the children might feel unhappy. Do they feel unhappy when they have to face new situations? Provide possible scenarios. For example, are they shy about making new friends? How did they feel when they went to school for the first time? Did they know anyone in their class before?

- Spend time talking about strategies for overcoming shyness or loneliness that can lead to unhappiness. Similarly, talk with children about ways of cheering themselves up. For example, do they have favorite toys that they like to cuddle when they are unhappy?

- Now talk about the things that might make adults unhappy. For example, would they be sad if a pet got lost or a friend moved away? What could they do to make themselves feel better?

- Take the opportunity to talk about welcoming new children to school. How could the children help them settle in so that they feel happy in their new school?

- Look at the picture story. Ask children to draw pictures of what makes them feel better when they are unhappy.

25

Library of Congress Cataloging-in-Publication Data
Graves, Sue, 1950–
   I'm not happy / written by Sue Graves ; illustrated by Desideria Guicciardini.
      p. cm. — (Our emotions and behavior)
   ISBN 978-1-57542-373-9
   1. Sadness in children—Juvenile literature. 2. Kindness—Juvenile literature. I. Guicciardini, Desideria, ill. II. Title.
III. Title: I am not happy.
   BF723.S15.G73 2011
   152.4—dc22
                                         2011001565

Reading Level Grades 1–2; Interest Level Ages 4–8; Fountas & Pinnell Guided Reading Level H

10 9 8 7 6 5 4 3 2 1
Printed in China
S14100311

Free Spirit Publishing Inc.
217 Fifth Avenue North, Suite 200
Minneapolis, MN 55401-1299
(612) 338-2068
help4kids@freespirit.com
www.freespirit.com

First published in 2011 by Franklin Watts, a division of Hachette Children's Books · London, UK, and Sydney, Australia

Text © Franklin Watts 2011
Illustrations © Desideria Guicciardini 2011

The rights of Sue Graves to be identified as the author and Desideria Guicciardini as the illustrator of this Work have
been asserted in accordance with the Copyright, Designs and Patents Act, 1988.

Editors: Adrian Cole and Jackie Hamley
Designers: Jonathan Hair and Peter Scoulding